Storyline Scotland

Book 2 by Moira Small

Oliver & Boyd

Language consultant for the series, Glenys M. Smith

Acknowledgments

We are grateful to the following for supplying photographs and information and giving permission for their use: Britoil plc, pp. 56, 61; Controller of Her Majesty's Stationery Office, p. 24; Edinburgh Wax Museum, p. 55; Peter Maxwell Stuart of Traquair, p. 33 (two); National Galleries of Scotland, pp. 44, 45, 115; Scottish Tourist Board, cover and pp. 7, 12, 26, 29, 36, 68, 128; Sportapic Sports Agency, p. 100; SRU and Scottish Rugby Clubs, p. 108; The British Petroleum Co. Ltd., p. 58, The Scotsman Publications Ltd., p. 103, Michael Wolchover, p. 64.

Illustrated by Rowan Clifford, John Harrold, Nicholas Hewetson, Annabel Large, Maggie Ling, Rob Norman, Jim Russell, Andrew Seir.

Oliver & Boyd
Robert Stevenson House
1–3 Baxter's Place
Leith Walk
Edinburgh EH1 3BB

A Division of Longman Group Ltd

ISBN 0 05 003563 0

First published 1985

Set in 14/20pt Monophoto Plantin
Produced by Longman Group (FE) Ltd
Printed in Hong Kong

Contents

The Goodman of Ballengeich

James V of Scotland was a good king. He liked to wander about his kingdom pretending to be an ordinary man. He often dressed up as a farmer.

One day he was walking near a farm called Braehead, near Edinburgh. He crossed Cramond Brig. Four men were hiding underneath the bridge. They jumped out at him and attacked him. They kicked him and hit him. They threw him to the ground and kicked him again.

A man working in a field near by heard the
commotion and ran to see if he could help.
When the men heard him coming they ran away.

The farm worker took King James
(although he did not know he was the King)
to the farmhouse. He gave him a basin of
water and a clean towel. He helped him
recover from the shock of being beaten up.
He gave him some water to drink.

"My name is Jock Howieson," said the
farm worker. "What's your name?"

"I am called 'The Goodman of
Ballengeich'," said the King. "I would like to
reward you for what you have done today.
You have saved my life."

"It was a pleasure, sir," said Jock Howieson. "I couldn't just watch a poor man get beaten up."

"Well then, tell me what you would like best in the whole world?" the King asked him.

Jock Howieson thought for a moment and then he said, "What I'd like best in the whole world would be to own a piece of land myself."

"I'll see what I can do about that," said the King. "I'm a servant of King James. Will you come to Holyrood Palace and see me again next week?"

Jock Howieson agreed. The following week he got all dressed up in his best clothes and went to Holyrood Palace. King James met him at the gate. Together they walked round the Palace. Jock Howieson thought it was beautiful. The King showed him all the rooms, then said, "Would you like to meet the King?"

"Oh, yes, I would, but he might be angry that I'm here," said Jock Howieson.

"I don't think so at all," said the King. "Come on, I'll take you to the Great Hall and you can meet him there."

"But how will I know the King?" asked Jock Howieson nervously.

"He'll be the only one wearing a hat," said King James.

So together they went into the Great Hall. Jock Howieson looked round at all the noblemen there. Not one of them was wearing a hat.

"It's either you or me," said Jock

Howieson, "for we are the only two wearing hats."

The King smiled. "Yes, Jock," he said. "I'm the King."

Jock Howieson was quite overwhelmed. He knelt down in front of King James. "Your Majesty," he said humbly.

"Get up, get up," said King James. "And thank you for saving my life last week. As a reward I will make you Laird of Braehead Farm."

"Oh thank you, sir, thank you very much," said Jock Howieson. "I can never thank you enough."

"There's no need," said the King. "But I do have one condition."

"What's that?" asked Jock Howieson.

"It is this," the King replied. "Every time the King passes you must come to him with a basin of water and a clean towel for him to use before he goes on his way."

"I agree to the condition," said Jock Howieson, smiling.

And he did. King James often went to see Jock Howieson, and they became good friends. There was always a basin of water and a clean towel ready, in case the royal visitor should arrive.

Jock Howieson farmed the Braehead land until he was an old man, and lived happily there all his days.

The Crown Jewels

Mairi was nervous. Mrs Grainger helped her to put the basket on the donkey's back.

"Come on, Mairi," she said. "It's time to go. Remember to walk slowly, just as we usually do."

"Oh, dear," said Mairi. "My knees are shaking!"

"So are mine," said Mrs Grainger. "But come on now, we'll be all right, you'll see."

Together they set off for the beach as usual. Mairi led the donkey and Mrs Grainger walked beside her. Mrs Grainger was the minister's wife and Mairi's job was to help her in the manse and garden. Most days they chatted happily, but today they were silent.

Mairi could see the soldiers' camp on the grass above the beach. For once she hoped they wouldn't see her. Today the two women would go along the beach as they often did, gathering seaweed to make soup, on their way

to Dunnottar Castle. Every day when they
went past the soldiers' camp they talked to
them and laughed at their jokes.

The soldiers were camping there waiting to
capture the Castle. They were in Oliver
Cromwell's army and he was the enemy of
the King. But Mairi had not thought much
about that until today.

"Today is different," she thought. "Today
we have to walk right round to the seaward
side of the Castle. Then we have to give the
signal to lower the basket. No one must see it
coming down to us, or . . ." And Mairi,
usually a sensible girl, shivered at the thought
of what might happen if the basket was seen.

Dunnottar Castle

They came to the top of the path by the beach.

"Oh dear," Mairi thought, "I *am* scared. What if someone sees the basket on its way down? What if the soldiers notice something unusual in the basket? What if . . .?" She shuddered at her thoughts.

"Do we really have to do this?" she asked Mrs Grainger. "Couldn't we go back to the house and try again tomorrow?"

"No, Mairi, no," said Mrs Grainger. "We'll have to do it. It's too important."

The two women had a difficult and dangerous task ahead of them. They were going to rescue the Crown Jewels of Scotland from Dunnottar Castle and take them away to safety.

The soldiers camping near the Castle were preparing for the attack. They were going to take the King's treasure. The people in the Castle were trapped. If any of them tried to escape they would be searched. But the soldiers had allowed Mrs Grainger and Mairi to go through their camp and right into the Castle.

Mrs Grainger was friendly with Mrs Ogilvie, the wife of the keeper of the Castle. Only the week before they had visited her and made a plan to rescue the Crown Jewels. They hoped that the soldiers would not suspect anything, because they walked along the beach nearly every day.

As they came near the camp Mrs Grainger said, "I hope the soldiers don't delay us, Mairi. Let's try and keep moving, shall we?"

"That's a good idea, but I see some of them watching us now," Mairi replied.

"Keep calm then," said Mrs Grainger. "We'll do the best we can."

Bravely the two women walked on.

"Hello there, it's a fine day!" said one of the soldiers.

"Aye, it is," said Mairi, but she kept walking. Mrs Grainger smiled and nodded to him but said nothing.

"You're surely in a hurry today?" he said.

"Och no, not really, it's just, well . . . we have a lot to do," said Mairi. Her voice trembled and she hoped he wouldn't notice.

"I hope I'll see you both again tomorrow," said the soldier, disappointed to see them go so quickly.

With relief they climbed right down on to the beach and began their task of collecting seaweed. They put it in the donkey's basket and worked their way along towards the Castle. The beach narrowed at the foot of a steep cliff where the Castle of Dunnottar towered above them.

Making sure no one was watching, they made their way round the face of the cliff, out of sight of the camp. Their skirts flapped in the wind and their hair blew in their eyes. Mairi's heart was thumping as she raised her scarf high above her head, like a flag, to signal that they were ready. They waited, but nothing happened. Then, suddenly, there was the basket! It swung on the end of a rope from a window high up in the Castle wall. The two women watched it coming down towards them. Once or twice it bumped into the cliff face, sending handfuls of stones rattling down.

Each time Mairi glanced round in alarm, but no one was there to see.

At last, with a little thud, the basket landed on the ground. They lifted out the contents with trembling hands.

"This must be the crown!" gasped Mairi, as she unwrapped the biggest bundle. The sun caught the sparkling jewels as she gazed at the crown. With great care she placed it gently at the bottom of the donkey's basket, under the seaweed.

"The sword is too big," whispered Mrs Grainger in alarm.

"What are we going to do?" asked Mairi.

"Let's try it without the scabbard,"

suggested Mrs Grainger. Mairi slid the
decorated scabbard off the sword and tried to
fit it into the donkey's basket.

"It's no good," said Mrs Grainger, "we'll
have to bend it." She put the sword across
her knee and tried to bend it in two. But she
wasn't strong enough.

"I'll give you a hand," said Mairi. "See,
we'll lay it across this rock and one of us can
lean on each end."

They did that. Slowly the great sword bent so that they were able to fit it into the basket on the donkey's back. The scabbard and the sceptre went in too. Then they carefully covered everything with seaweed.

Now the treasure basket was empty. Again Mairi waved her scarf high above her head as the signal for the basket to be pulled up. Then the two women began the long and dangerous walk back the way they had come.

The wind was strong and sand blew in their faces. Mairi held tight to the donkey's rein, and Mrs Grainger kept her hand on the basket in case the precious load slipped.

"Hello again!" said a voice. It was the same soldier. "You two look as if you've seen a ghost, you're both as white as a sheet!" he exclaimed.

"We're all right," said Mairi. "But you did give us a fright, suddenly appearing like that!"

"I certainly didn't mean to frighten you, especially after you've been working so hard. That's a lot of seaweed you've got there!"

"Yes, we have, haven't we?" stammered
Mairi.

"We're going to make a lot of soup tonight
for the poor people of the parish," said
Mrs Grainger quickly. "In this weather they
certainly need it. We must be getting along.
Good-day to you."

"Good-day to you, ma'am," said the
soldier with a smile. Mairi and Mrs Grainger
thankfully went walking on.

"See you tomorrow perhaps," called Mairi
as she turned and waved to him.

When they came to the end of the beach
they stopped for a short rest. The donkey ate
some grass and the two women sat down with

their backs against the rocks. Suddenly they heard footsteps in the sand. Too frightened to move, they sat very still. They heard men's voices behind them and caught snatches of a conversation.

"Tonight . . . we'll storm the keep . . ."

"Orders . . . Cromwell himself . . . the King's treasures . . ."

Peeping through a gap in the rocks, Mairi saw two officers striding by.

"Come on," said Mrs Grainger urgently, "let's be on our way."

Mairi grabbed the donkey's rein and started up the path. She did not stop or look behind until she reached the top.

"Not so fast," said Mrs Grainger. "We want this to look as if we're doing our usual stroll, remember?"

So they slowly walked the long miles back to the manse. When they got there they took the donkey into the shed and lifted the basket from its back. Carefully they brought the precious load into the kitchen. They

unpacked the Crown Jewels and Mrs Grainger
hid them in her bedroom, under the big
double bed!

Later, when the minister came home, they
told him all about their daring walk along the
beach. When they told him about the two
officers' conversation, he looked worried.

"We must hide the jewels tonight, in case
the soldiers come here," he said.

So when darkness had fallen and everyone else was in bed, the basket was filled again and the donkey, the two women and Mr Grainger made their way to the church at Kinneff. There they hid the Crown Jewels under the floor, in a space beneath the pulpit.

The jewels stayed there for nine years. No one told the secret of their rescue, and only Mr and Mrs Grainger and Mairi knew they were in the church. When all the danger was past they were taken back to Dunnottar Castle.

*   *   *   *   *

This is a true story which took place in the year 1651. Cromwell's soldiers did attack Dunnottar Castle and after some time they captured it. But when they searched for the Crown Jewels they couldn't find them.

The jewels were never found or given to the King's enemies because of the bravery of Mrs Grainger and Mairi that day on the beach.

*   *   *   *   *

If you would like to see the Crown Jewels of Scotland, they are in a special room in Edinburgh Castle called the Crown Room. They are guarded night and day by a man called 'The Warden of the Regalia', who has

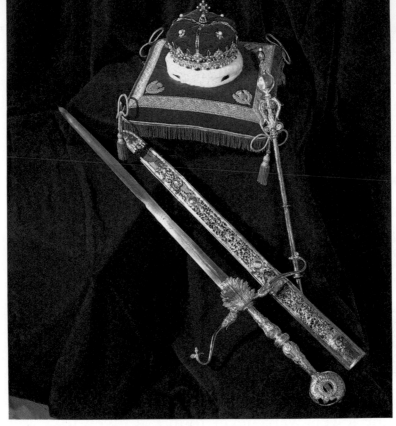

The Crown Jewels of Scotland

fourteen soldiers to help him. If anyone tries
to steal the jewels, alarms go off and the
doors and windows of the Crown Room are
sealed immediately.

If you look carefully at the sword you can
see where it was damaged when Mrs Grainger
and Mairi bent it to fit into their donkey's
basket.

Burglary in the Borders

Ian liked collecting things. He collected
postcards and stamps. He collected car
registration numbers and comics, especially
space comics. Wherever he went he collected
things.

"I can't think why you collect all that
junk," said his mother. "It's no use to man or
beast!"

But Ian went on collecting things in spite
of what she said.

One day in the summer holidays he went in
the car with his mother and her friend to
Traquair House.

His mother's friend was called Jennifer. She came from the United States. She wore brightly-coloured clothes and a jangly bracelet and she smelled of perfume. She kept saying, "Isn't it *wonderful?*"

On the way there Ian's mother told Jennifer about Traquair House. "It's a lovely old country house, the oldest inhabited house in Scotland."

Traquair House. The present Laird is Mr Peter Maxwell Stuart, whose ancestors have been there since the 15th century.

They came to the bridge over the River
Tweed, crossed it and drove in through the
gates of Traquair House. They parked the car
beside a rusty Renault and a bright blue
Allegro. Ian noticed that the Allegro had a
damaged number plate, but he wrote the
number down anyway. It was FGB 764X.
Then he put the notebook in his pocket.

A man stood at the door collecting tickets.
They went inside and looked round. The
rooms were filled with china, furniture and
pictures.

By the time they reached the drawing-room
upstairs Jennifer had said 'Isn't it *wonderful?*'
eight times altogether. Ian was counting.

At the top of the stairs there was an antique shop. Ian knew that Jennifer and his mother would take a long time in there.

"I'll just go and have a look round on my own for a bit," he told them.

He made his way along a corridor. He noticed a row of interesting pictures hanging on the wall. There were four altogether. Ian liked them.

He came to the library. There were books lining the walls right up to the ceiling. Then he came to a bedroom known as the King's Room.

Ian found a little stairway leading from it, which he climbed to see what was up there. The stairs were steep and he was out of breath when he reached the top. He stepped out into a room full of glass cases with things to look at inside. There was a mural painted on the wall.

Suddenly Ian caught sight of a very old lady going towards the stairway. He watched her. She was carrying a large shopping bag.

"She's far too old to go down that way,"
he thought. "She'll fall. I'd better go over
and tell her how steep it is."

But when he got to the top of the stairs
there was no sign of her. Ian went down again
himself. She was nowhere to be seen. Feeling
puzzled, he went to find his mother and
Jennifer again.

"Ian!" said Jennifer. "Isn't it *wonderful?*"

Ian smiled at her and said to his mother, "Mum, come on, I want to show you the King's Room and the secret stair! Come on, I'll show you."

He led his mother along the corridor to the place where he had seen the pictures. Then he stared. Two of the pictures had gone!

"Mum!" he shouted. "Two of the pictures have been stolen!"

"Don't be daft, Ian," said his mother. "No one would take pictures off a wall in broad daylight."

"I think they might," said Ian. "And I think I know who took them, too! Mum, you go and tell someone, and I'll go and see if I can catch the thief."

Leaving his mother staring after him, Ian ran as fast as he could out of the house and towards the car park. He got there just in time to see the Allegro with the damaged number plate disappearing through the main gates. It was going very fast. The old lady

whom he had seen at the secret stair was
driving.

Then he heard his mother calling. "Ian,
come back here, will you?" He ran back to
his mother who was standing beside the ticket
collector.

"Two of your old pictures have been
stolen!" Ian said. "Can you phone the
police?" Then he added, "I've got the thief's
car number here!"

The ticket man telephoned the police. Ian
gave them a description of the car and its
number: FGB 764X. The police stopped the
car at the Border not far away. The old lady
Ian had seen was really a man in disguise.

The two pictures were found unharmed in the boot of the car, hidden under a travelling rug.

"Well done, Ian, excellent work!" said one of the policemen.

"Thank you very, very much indeed," said the ticket collector.

"We are most grateful to you," said the owner of the house.

Jennifer put her arms round Ian and said, "Everything in Scotland is just wonderful ... *and so are you*!"

"That's the eighteenth time you've said that today," Ian told her.

"Ian, don't be rude!" said his mother. "All the same," she added, "your collecting certainly was useful for once."

The bed in the King's Room which you can see in the picture is said to have been used by Mary Queen of Scots. She isn't the only royal to have sheltered within Traquair – over the centuries 27 kings and queens have stayed there. Try to find out who some of them were.

The library has in its collection a 14th century hand-painted Bible, and the Nuremberg Chronicle, printed in 1493. Books had to be hand-written before printing was developed. Who invented the printing press, and when?

You can visit the house from April to October. The address is Traquair House, Innerleithen, Peeblesshire EH44 6PW.

Lady Elizabeth Campbell

Long ago in Argyll there lived a beautiful lady. She was the daughter of the Chief of the Clan Campbell, whose home was Inveraray Castle. Her name was Lady Elizabeth Campbell. Everyone who knew her loved her, for she was kind and good as well as beautiful.

All of the time that Lady Elizabeth was growing up, the Campbells had been fighting the Macleans. It seemed that they would never stop. The battles were fierce and many men were killed. Elizabeth's father decided he must try to stop the fighting. He went to see Lachlan Maclean, the Chief of the Clan Maclean.

"It is my great desire that there should be peace between us," he said. "I'd like to offer you my daughter as peacemaker. She is beautiful and good, and will serve you well. If you agree, we'll arrange the marriage as soon as possible."

Lachlan Maclean agreed immediately, for
he was old, bad-tempered and ugly, and not
at all popular with the ladies.

When he reached home her father told
Lady Elizabeth about his decision.

"I've arranged that you will marry Lachlan
Maclean, Chief of the Clan Maclean, so that
we may have peace between us," he told her.

Lady Elizabeth was very, very upset.

"How can I marry that man?" she asked.
"I've already met the man I want to marry
. . . oh, please don't make me do such a thing!"
And she fell on her knees in front of
her father and cried and cried.

Inveraray Castle

"Come, come, my dear, it won't be as bad as that," her father said. "He lives in a fine castle, and we must make sure of an end to this dreadful fighting."

And so Lady Elizabeth married Lachlan Maclean and went to live with him at Duart Castle.

At first he was kind to her. But he wouldn't allow her to write to her family at Inveraray. He didn't want her to speak to them again. That made her sad. She often wondered how her father and brother were getting on without her.

Her only friend was her maid Mairi who had come with her from Inveraray.

After a year a baby boy was born to her and that made her feel much happier. One day, not long after the baby had been born, Mairi came rushing in.

"There are some visitors to see you," she said. "We'd better keep it a secret or there'll be trouble!"

Just then, two handsome young men strode into the room. One was Lady Elizabeth's brother. The other was his friend, the man she had wanted so much to marry.

"We've been so worried about you," said her brother. "We haven't heard a thing from you since you left home."

So Lady Elizabeth explained to them that her husband wouldn't allow her to write to them. She told them she was fine and proudly showed them her baby boy.

Just then Mairi came in. "Lachlan Maclean is coming over the hill. Come quickly or there'll be trouble! I'll show you a back way out."

The two young men hurried off to their boat and sailed away. They thought no one had seen them, but they were wrong. They had been seen by an old cow-herd called Duncan. He well remembered the fights with the Campbells and thought he might stir up a bit of trouble. So he told as many people as he could that Lady Elizabeth had had two strange men visiting her. It was not long before someone went to Lachlan Maclean and told him.

By this time he had grown tired of having such a gentle lady for his wife. He ordered his servants to get rid of her, and then he set off on a hunting trip.

Soon after he left, two rough men came and grabbed Lady Elizabeth and forced her down to the beach. They pushed her into a boat and rowed out to sea. She begged them to take her back to the shore. She wept and called for mercy. But the men refused to listen. Instead they left her stranded on a tiny rocky island, knowing that the tide would

soon come up and she would drown.

Poor Lady Elizabeth was terrified and very
cold. She shouted for help until she was
hoarse but no one came. There was no one to
hear her calls.

Just by chance a fisherman in a boat a long
way off thought he saw something fluttering
on a rock in the distance. When he came
nearer he saw that a woman was stranded
there. The tide was coming in fast and he
reached her just in time to save her.

The fisherman wrapped an old cloak round
her and took her to the shore. He made her as
comfortable as he could and went off to find
help. On his way he met a young man, and

told him of the beautiful woman he had saved from drowning. Together they went back to find Lady Elizabeth. The man turned out to be her brother! Imagine how shocked and horrified he was to hear what had happened.

He took her to her father's home at Inveraray, where everyone was happy to see her. She was glad to be back. But her baby son was still at Duart Castle. She was worried about him and she was worried about Mairi, too. So plans were made for Mairi and the baby to be rescued.

The next day a messenger arrived from Duart. He brought a letter from Lachlan Maclean telling of the tragic death of Lady Elizabeth. The letter said that she had died in her husband's arms.

Lady Elizabeth's father was furious! However he sent the messenger back to Lachlan Maclean with an invitation for him to come to Inveraray and tell the sad tale himself.

So Lachlan Maclean made the journey to Inveraray Castle.

When he arrived he was surprised to see
the flags flying and to smell good things to
eat. The Chief of the Clan Campbell met him
at the gate. Lachlan told the sad story of the
death of his wife.

Then he learned that there was to be a
feast to celebrate the arrival of a new mistress
at Inveraray.

When Lachlan Maclean saw the feast table
laid with its silver candlesticks and fine linen,

he wished he was still married to Lady
Elizabeth after all. Her family must be very rich
to own such beautiful things.

In came the Chief with an elegant lady in a
long satin dress. She wore a veil over her face
and no one could recognise her. Lachlan
Maclean thought she looked very grand. At
the end of the meal he jumped to his feet to
propose a toast to the lady.

"A toast," he cried, "to the health and
happiness of the beautiful and mysterious
lady, the new mistress of Inveraray!"

As he raised his glass Lady Elizabeth drew
back her veil. Lachlan Maclean gasped. His

glass fell to the floor. He saw that it was his wife. He was terrified.

"Here is the new mistress of Inveraray. You left her to die at the mercy of the tide," said her father grimly.

Lachlan Maclean began to slink away. But Lady Elizabeth's brother shouted, "Oh, no, Maclean, NO . . . you and I must fight, for no man treats MY sister like that!"

A fierce fight took place in front of the castle. At the end, Lachlan Maclean lay dead on the ground.

Just then came the sound of horses' hooves. It was Mairi and the baby safely home.

Lady Elizabeth was very happy. However, she did not stay long at Inveraray. She married the man she had always wanted to marry, and went to live with him in England. There they prospered and had four more children.

Adapted

Burke and Hare

This is a true horror story.

Once there lived two cruel and greedy men. Their names were William Burke and William Hare. They lived in the city of Edinburgh in the nineteenth century.

At that time, Edinburgh was a dangerous place at night. The streets were badly lit, and robbers and murderers lurked in the shadows of the closes, ready to pounce on innocent victims.

Burke's
lodging house

A = Burke's
window

B = Back
entrance

William Burke   William Hare

Burke and Hare had come from Ireland in search of work. They sometimes worked on farms near the city walls. Burke also worked as manager of a lodging house near Tanner's Close in the old part of the city. Hare helped him to look after the people who came to the lodging house.

One night an old man came to stay. In the morning, Burke knocked on the door of his room. He was afraid that the old man might have left without paying for his lodging.

"Time to get up, old man," he said. There was no reply, so Burke went into the room. He found the old man still in bed. Burke tried to wake him. But the old man had died in his sleep during the night.

Burke called out to his friend, Hare.

"Look what we have here," he said. "The old man's dead and he hasn't paid for his board and lodging!"

"There may be money in his pockets," said Hare, rummaging through the old man's belongings. "Nothing at all," he said, shaking his head.

Burke caught Hare's arm and, as if the old man could still hear him, whispered, "Let's sell his body to the medical school behind the Royal Infirmary. The students need bodies, I've heard, for their anatomy lessons."

"We can't do that!" said Hare.

"Why not?" asked Burke. "He hasn't paid us. He owes us money."

"But the poor old soul needs a proper burial," said Hare.

"No one will know," said Burke, "and we'll get a lot of money for the body."

Reluctantly Hare agreed. Together they went to see the man at the medical school about the sale of the body. "I'll give you ten

pounds for a fresh body in good condition,"
said the man.

So that night Burke and Hare dragged the
old man's body down the back stairs of the
lodging house and lifted it on to their cart.
They covered it up with an old grey blanket
and tucked it in all the way round.

"Just think," said Burke to Hare, "we're
going to be rich!"

The man at the medical school gave them
ten pounds. Burke and Hare were very
pleased with themselves. The next day
they sat down for a talk.

"We'll have to get some more bodies to sell," said Burke.

"Where from?" asked Hare in amazement.

"We could dig them up," suggested Burke.

"Oh, I couldn't do that," said Hare with a shiver. "I'd be scared stiff in the graveyard in the middle of the night!"

"You're not only lazy," said Burke scornfully, "you're a coward too!"

"Well," said Hare, "maybe we could have another, er, um, unexpected death at the lodging house. I mean we could help someone to die a little sooner ... couldn't we?" And he smiled slyly.

"I see what you mean," said Burke. "That really is a good idea." And he nodded approvingly at Hare.

So that night Burke and Hare served drinks to the customers as usual. But they made sure that one old woman drank more than she should. They kept filling her glass whenever it was empty. By the end of the evening she had fallen asleep in the corner of the room.

When all the other customers had gone
home Burke brought the old grey blanket.
He put it over the old woman's face and
smothered her. Later that night they took her
body to the medical school. In exchange they
received another ten pounds.

For many weeks after that they plotted and
schemed to get more bodies. A number of
people disappeared from the streets of
Edinburgh and were never seen again. During

that time Burke and Hare took sixteen bodies to the medical school. They were delighted because they were making so much money. But they began to be careless.

One dark night, when they were wheeling a body along in their cart, they were seen by some young men who were going home late from a party.

"What are they up to?" said one of the young men.

"Let's follow them and see," said another.

So they did. They followed Burke and Hare all the way to the medical school. They watched them deliver the body at the back door. Then they watched the two rogues run home chuckling, the money jingling in their pockets.

The next evening two of the young men who had followed them went to the lodging house where Burke and Hare worked. They sat in a corner of the room, eating and drinking like the rest of the customers.

They watched Hare serving an old man

drink when he hadn't ordered it. They
noticed that the old man became drowsy.
When it was time for everyone else to leave,
they noticed that the old man was fast asleep.
No one paid any attention to him but left
him lying there.

Suspicious, the two young men waited
outside to see what would happen. They
waited for an hour, then another. They got
tired and cold, so they decided to go home.
But just then they heard a sound. They hid
in the close near by.

Burke and Hare came out of the lodging house dragging the body of an old man. The two young men were certain it was the same old man they had seen drinking earlier. They watched in horror as Burke and Hare loaded the body on to the cart.

They followed them all the way to the medical school. They saw them hand over the body and watched as they ran home with the money in their pockets.

The next day they went to the magistrate and told him what they had seen.

By the end of that week Burke and Hare had been arrested. At their trial it was difficult to prove that they had committed the crimes of murdering all those people. Those who had died seemed to have died from natural causes. There were no marks on any of the bodies. But it was extremely suspicious that so many bodies had been taken to the medical school in such a short time.

Then a medical student came forward to give evidence. He told the court that he had been given a body to work with. He found, to his horror, that it was the body of a man he had known. Even worse, he had seen and talked with him the day before!

Hare denied killing the man. Burke backed him up. There was still no real evidence. Then a clever lawyer came forward to ask some questions. "What happened to Mary Paterson?" he asked.

Burke was so surprised that the lawyer knew the name of one of their victims that he started to panic. "Hare killed her, sir!" he shouted. "Hare killed her in self defence! You see, she wouldn't pay for her drinks."

Hare jumped to his feet. He was furious that Burke had told a tale on him. He began to shout out the whole story. He told the court about the first body and the old man who had died in his sleep. He told how he hadn't really wanted to get any more bodies. He confessed that he was greedy for the money. In the end he told the whole dreadful story.

Burke was sentenced to death. Hare was to be imprisoned.

Burke was hanged in the High Street beside the Mercat Cross. It was the year 1829. Hare managed to escape from his jailers. He ran for his life. Many people pursued him but he got away, and was never seen again in Edinburgh.

Since that time laws have been passed to protect the public from such happenings. People can make wills to say that they wish to donate their bodies when they die to medical research. Medical students still need to study anatomy.

If you visit the Wax Museum in Edinburgh you can see wax models of Burke and Hare. They are in the Chamber of Horrors. I am sure you will agree that that is the best place for them!

Joe and Jim

Once there were two friends called Joe and Jim. They were off-shore workers on an oil rig in the North Sea. Most of the time they got along well together, although they were quite different.

Joe was fat and Jim was thin. Joe was dark and Jim was fair. Joe always worked on the night shift. Jim always worked on the day shift.

They shared a bedroom on the oil rig. It was a comfortable room with a place to hang clothes, a desk, a telephone and two bunk beds.

Joe slept in the top bunk. Jim slept in the bottom bunk. The only trouble was that neither Joe nor Jim could get a good night's sleep in the bunk beds.

They spent two weeks at a time aboard the oil rig. That's a long time to go without a proper sleep. By the end of the two weeks they both got very cross.

"This bed is too hard for me," grumbled Joe.

"This bed is too soft for me," grumbled Jim.

"This bed is too high up for me," grumbled Joe.

"This bed is too low down for me," grumbled Jim.

Joe worked in the central control room of the oil rig all night long. He spent his time checking and double-checking all the meters and dials in the control room. He had to write down a record of what they said. One

Control room of a rig in BP's Forties oilfield in the North Sea

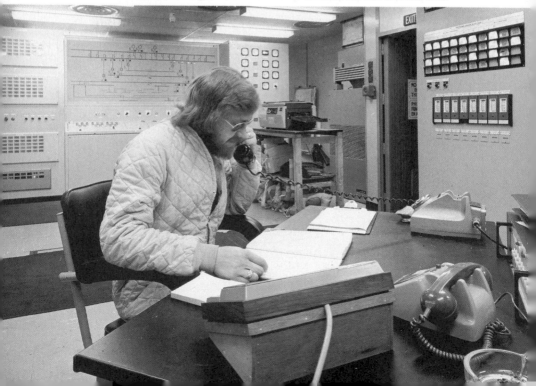

night, near the end of his shift, he began to
make mistakes. He wrote down the wrong
numbers in his book. He had to change them
and go back three times to make sure he had
it right.

At the end of his shift he went to find Jim,
who was eating his breakfast in the dining
room. He was having bacon and eggs and a
mug of tea.

"Jim, I'm really worried," Joe said. "I
can't concentrate properly. I'll have to find a
way of getting more sleep while I'm here."

"Try not to worry, Joe," said Jim kindly.
"Why don't you go and see your doctor when
you get home? Maybe he'll give you some
sleeping pills."

"Good idea," said Joe. He sat down and
ate his breakfast too.

Jim went off to do his work. He was a
platform attendant. He had to unload the
supplies that came to the rig by sea, and
make sure that they were delivered to the
right place.

One day a massive box of cornflakes was unloaded. Jim made sure it was taken to the kitchen. Another day a huge box of paper and a new typewriter arrived. Jim made sure they were taken to the office.

Sometimes Jim unloaded the new films. He took them along to the cinema. There was a different film every evening on the rig. Jim liked going to the cinema. But that day he didn't feel very well at the end of his shift.

"I'll just have a lie down for a while," he thought. He went to his room and lay down on his bunk. He had a pain in his tummy. It got worse and worse.

Joe, lying in the bunk above him, sat up. "What's wrong, Jim?" he asked.

"Send for the doctor, Joe," groaned Jim. "I've got a terrible pain."

Joe jumped down from his bunk, and telephoned for the doctor. "Can you send the doctor immediately, please?"

"Try not to worry, Jim," Joe said. "The doctor will be here in a minute." He looked

at Jim. He was pale and ill-looking and he was clutching his tummy.

The doctor came and examined Jim. "Hospital. Straight away," he said.

Within minutes Jim was strapped to a stretcher and carefully lifted aboard a waiting helicopter. Joe watched it take off and waved until it had disappeared into the evening sky.

All of a sudden Joe felt weary. He went back to his room and lay down on Jim's bed.

"My goodness, this is comfortable!" he said. "I must sleep here tonight!" So he did. It was the best sleep he had ever had since going to work on the rig.

In the morning there was a message to tell him that Jim had had his appendix out. He would be fine in a few days. Joe was dclighted.

Two days later a helicopter came to take him and the rest of the men off the rig and home to the mainland for two weeks' leave.

Joe decided to visit Jim in hospital. He bought a bunch of grapes and a bottle of orange juice to take with him. He found Jim sitting up in bed looking much better.

"Hello there, Jim," said Joe. "How are you feeling now?"

"Much better, thanks," said Jim. "Thanks very much for all you did to help. The doctor says they got me here in the nick of time."

"Not at all," said Joe. "You would have done exactly the same for me."

"I hope so," said Jim. "But is there anything I can do for you, when I'm out of here, to thank you?"

"Well," said Joe, "there is one thing."

"What's that?" asked Jim.

Joe told him. "Do you think you and I could swop bunks when we get back to the rig next time?"

Jim leaned forward and said quietly, "I'm so glad you asked first. I've found this hospital bed so comfortable – it's hard and it's high up, you see. I came to the conclusion that I'd sleep better on the top bunk. So I was going to ask you the very same thing!"

"That's settled then," said Joe, "and the sooner you're back the better."

Jim was soon back to work on the rig. He and Joe shared the room again, but this time Joe slept in the bottom bunk and Jim slept in the top one. They slept so well that they were never grumpy again, and they did their work so well that they got promotion and earned lots and lots of money!

Find a map showing oil fields on the 'United Kingdom Continental Shelf' – as the sea area around the British Isles is called. You can see why oil rig workers have to rely on helicopters ... a boat would take too long to get back to land in an emergency, or when the workers go on leave!

Britoil is one of the big companies looking for oil and gas in the North Sea. It is involved in nine oil fields, with two terminals to bring the oil ashore, Nigg Bay in the Cromarty Firth and Sullom Voe in the Shetland Islands.

This table shows how deep the water is at each Britoil rig. You can imagine how long the drill will have to be to reach the sea-bed! Draw a graph to compare the depths, starting with the deepest, which is Thistle.

Can you find these oil fields on your map? Add other fields to your graph, using a different colour for those explored by other companies, if possible.

OIL FIELDS	WATER DEPTH
Beatrice	46 m
Clyde	79 m
Dunlin	152 m
Hutton	146 m
Murchison	152 m
Ninian	149 m
South Brae	113 m
Statfjord	145 m
Thistle	162 m

The Flitting

Julie lived in Glasgow with her Mum and
Dad. She liked living in their street. Every
day after school she played with her friends
Joan and Sharon. They played with their
skipping ropes, and sometimes they played
hide and seek.

But one day Julie's Mum told her that they
would have to move house. All the houses in
their street were going to be knocked down.
New ones were going to be built in their place.

The day of the flitting arrived. Uncle Bob came in his van. He parked it outside Julie's house. He and Julie's Dad loaded all the things from the house into the van. Julie helped Mum pack up the last of the things to take to the new house.

"Bring the kettle over here, Julie," said Mum. "And stop worrying. It'll be OK."

"I don't want to leave my friends," said Julie. "What if there's no one in the new flats to be friends with?"

"There's bound to be *someone*, Julie," said Mum. "After all, the flats are eighteen storeys high!"

They looked round to make sure they hadn't left anything behind.

"Tomorrow the bulldozers will be here to knock it down," thought Julie. She walked sadly to the door.

"Can't say I'm sorry to go!" said Mum briskly, as she closed the door behind them. She and Julie climbed up into the van beside Uncle Bob and Dad. The van moved off down the street.

Julie waved to her friends. "Cheerio, Joan!" she called. "Cheerio, Sharon, cheerio everybody!"

A tear ran down her cheek. "Cheerio, street," she whispered. Mum put her arm round her.

"It'll be OK, Julie, you'll see," said Mum.

A little while later they arrived at the foot of the high-rise flats. Julie jumped down from the van and stood looking up at them. She had to tilt her head right back to see to the very top.

"Up you go, you two," said Dad.

Mum and Julie went up in one of the lifts. Mum pressed the button for the tenth floor and up they went. Julie watched the light go on at each landing, showing the floor they were on.

"Children aren't supposed to use the lifts on their own," said Mum. "Remember that, mind."

"Yes, Mum," said Julie. She didn't think she would like to go in the lifts by herself anyway.

When they reached the tenth floor the lift stopped. They got out.

"This one is ours," said Mum, crossing the landing to a bright yellow door.

There were two other doors on the landing. Julie wondered who lived there. Mum showed her round the new flat. There was a bedroom for Julie and one for Mum and Dad. There was a sitting room and a kitchen with a space to put the table and chairs.

"It's great!" said Julie. "I can't wait to get everything up here."

"Same here," said Mum.

"I'll go and see if Dad's coming," said Julie. She went out on to the landing again but there was no sign of Dad. Over in the corner Julie saw another door. She found that it led onto a balcony. Holding on to the railing, she gazed at the view.

In the distance she could see the Clyde shipyards. She could see the dry dock where Dad sometimes worked. Far below she could see the cars and Uncle Bob's van. They looked like toys from this height. A voice behind her made her turn round.

"Hello, I'm Jenny," said a girl about Julie's age. "I live next door to you in the flat with the blue door. I came to tell you there's a power cut. All the lifts are off. Mum wanted to let you know."

Julie liked the look of Jenny. She smiled at her. "Thanks very much," she said. "Come on, we'll go and tell my Mum."

"Oh, dear," said Julie's Mum when they told her. "That's just like the thing."

She sent Julie all the way down by the stairs to tell Uncle Bob and Dad what had happened. Jenny went with Julie. It was a long way downstairs. When they reached the bottom Uncle Bob was unloading the van by himself.

"There's a power cut," said Julie.

"All the lifts are off," said Jenny.

Uncle Bob looked at them. Then he laughed. "Trust your Dad!" he said and shook his head. "He must be stuck somewhere on the way up!" Then he laughed again. "He'll be OK. He's got the budgie with him for company, and an armchair to sit on . . . and my paper in his pocket!''

The three of them went to the lift door. Uncle Bob pressed the button beside the door. No light came on. Uncle Bob scratched his head.

"Now what?" he asked himself.

"There's a wee window on all the lift doors," said Jenny.

"Well, see if you can find your Dad. It's worth a try," said Uncle Bob. "I'll stay here and unload some more stuff."

Julie and Jenny set off up the stairs. They looked through the window on the lift door on the first floor. They could see nothing but darkness. They looked through the window on the lift door on the second floor. They could see nothing but darkness there either. They looked through the window on the lift door on the third floor.

This time, as they peered in through the window, they saw Dad peering out! He made a funny face at them. He said something, but

they couldn't hear him.

"Let's go and get Uncle Bob," said Julie.

Down they went again and found Uncle
Bob. He came back up the stairs with them to
the place where the lift was stuck. He tried to
open the lift door but it wouldn't move. He
tried pressing the button beside the door but
nothing happened. He shook his head at Dad
through the glass. Dad made a thumbs down
sign and shrugged his shoulders. He looked
quite dismal shut in there.

"Nothing else for it," said Uncle Bob. "We'll just carry the stuff up ourselves."

"All that way!" said Jenny.

"Just you and me and Jenny?" asked Julie.

"Well, we could just make a start," said Uncle Bob. He gave Dad a cheery wave and set off again down to the van.

There were two punk rockers standing looking at the van. They were both chewing gum. "Flitting, eh?" said one.

"That's right," said Uncle Bob. "How about giving us a hand? The lifts are off and we don't know when they'll be fixed. We thought we'd take some things up by the stairs."

"Which floor?" asked the punk rocker with orange hair.

"Tenth," Julie told her.

"Could have been the eighteenth!" said the one with pink hair, and laughed at her own joke.

They each lifted a large box and set off towards the stairway. Julie followed, carrying a boxful of things for her own room. Jenny came behind her with Mum's cushions in a big plastic bag. Uncle Bob took the coffee table.

The strange procession plodded up the stairs. When they reached the third floor they stopped for a minute and waved to Dad. He looked amazed when he saw the punk rockers.

When they reached the tenth floor they were hot and very tired.

"Dad's stuck in the lift," Julie told Mum.

"Trust him," she said, "to miss his own flitting!"

They put their things down inside the flat.

"Let's go for another load," said Uncle Bob.

"Why not?" said the punk rockers, and they set off down the stairs. Julie and Jenny followed and so did Uncle Bob.

When they arrived at the van a policeman was standing looking at it. "Flitting, are you?" he asked Uncle Bob.

"That's right," said Uncle Bob. "These

girls are giving us a hand. There's a power cut, you see, and the lifts aren't working. We're taking everything up by the stairs."

"I'll give you a hand," said the policeman. "I have to go up to the eleventh floor anyway."

Uncle Bob handed him the TV set! He gave the punk rockers a rolled-up carpet to carry between them. Julie took a case full of clothes. Jenny took a box filled with sheets and pillowcases. Uncle Bob lifted an armchair by its legs. And off they all went up the stairs.

They were glad to have a rest on the third floor. They waved to Dad who looked very surprised to see two punk rockers and a policeman helping them. Then they went all the way up to the tenth floor.

Mum was delighted to see all the things they had brought. Jenny's Mum had made a cup of tea. So they all had some tea before they went down to the van again.

When they got back to the van Julie was surprised to see her friend Joan standing there. When she saw Julie coming, Joan began to hop up and down in excitement.

"Julie!" she said. "My Mum and Dad have the chance of a flat on the twelfth floor. We've come to see it. Maybe we'll be neighbours again!"

"That's great!" said Julie. "This is Jenny. She lives in the flat next door to our new one. She'll be a neighbour too."

Then Joan's Mum and Dad came along. "Hello, Julie, how's the flitting going?" they asked.

Julie explained about the power cut and the lifts being off and Dad being stuck on the third floor. She told them that they were taking everything up by the stairs. Joan's Mum and Dad offered to help too.

"After all," said Joan's Mum, "we want to get to the twelfth floor to see our flat."

Julie and Jenny and Joan set off carrying a kitchen chair each. The two punk rockers both took an end of the kitchen table. Joan's Mum and Dad took a mattress between them. Uncle Bob took Mum's sewing machine. Dad looked astonished when he saw the procession of people going past his lift window.

All afternoon they toiled up and down the stairs. All afternoon Dad remained shut in the lift.

"One more box and that's it," announced Uncle Bob at last. "I'll go down for it myself." Off he went, leaving the rest of them to help Mum unpack the boxes and put things away.

When Uncle Bob reached the third floor it was his turn for a surprise. The lift door opened and out came Dad.

"The power must be back on again at last," he said. "The lift door suddenly opened. I thought I would be in there for ever."

"Let's go down in the lift then," said Uncle Bob.

"Not on your life!" said Dad. "I've been in there too long. I'd rather walk."

"Right," said Uncle Bob. "I'll go down in the lift and meet you at the bottom. In fact I'll race you!"

Dad ran down the stairs as fast as he could. But Uncle Bob was standing at the bottom when he got there.

"We'll put the last box in the lift," said Uncle Bob thankfully.

"Why not?" said Dad. "You go on up with it. I'm going to the fish and chip van to buy everybody some tea!"

So Uncle Bob went up in the lift with the last box. A few minutes after him Dad arrived, laden with fish and chips all wrapped in newspaper.

They all sat round the kitchen table. It was a bit crowded but it was great fun. The punk rockers had fish and chips and mealy pudding. The policeman had haggis and fish

and chips. Joan's Mum and Dad had fish
suppers. Julie's Mum and Jenny's Mum had
fish only, because they were slimming. Uncle
Bob and Dad had the biggest helpings of fish
and chips Julie had ever seen.

It was just like a party. When everybody
had gone Julie and her Mum and Dad made
up the beds. Julie wondered why she had
been so worried that morning.

"What a flitting!" she thought as she climbed into bed.

Dad came through to tuck her in and say goodnight. "What a flitting!" he said.

Mum came through to tuck her in as well. "What a flitting, Julie!" she said.

Julie snuggled down into her own bed in their new flat and thought, "I'm going to like it here. And I'm going to play with Jenny and Joan on the landing tomorrow." Then she fell fast asleep.

The Tobermory Legend

Long ago there lived a proud and beautiful lady. She lived with her husband and children in a castle built at the edge of the sea.

She had everything she wanted. She had fine clothes to wear. She had a cook and a housekeeper. She had four healthy children, two boys and two girls. Her husband loved her very much and made sure that she had everything in the world she wanted.

She should have been very happy. But she was discontented and cross instead. Every day she sat in her sitting room at the castle and ordered everyone about. They always did what she said.

One day a messenger came to the castle.

"Good-day," he said to the lady of the castle.

"Good-day to you," said she. "What news do you bring today?"

"News of a great ship, ma'am," he told her. "She sails into Tobermory today. She is the *Florencia*, a great galleon from the Spanish Armada. It is said that there is a Spanish princess aboard, as well as a treasure of gold in the hold!"

"Thank you for bringing this news," said the lady. "But it is of no interest to me."

The messenger left the room disappointed. On his way out, he met the lord of the castle.

"What brings you here today, young man?"
he asked the messenger.

"I bring news, sir, news of the Spanish
ship *Florencia*."

"Well then, tell me," said the lord. "Does
she approach our shores?"

"Indeed, sir, she will be in the bay at
Tobermory by night!"

"Thank you, young man, for bringing such
good news," said the lord, and he gave the
messenger a silver coin. The messenger left
the castle feeling much better after that.

Then the lord went in to see his wife.
"Have you heard the news about the
Florencia?" he asked her.

"I have heard the news," she said.

"Well, let us go now to Tobermory and see
the great ship tonight."

"But I don't want to do that," said the lady
crossly.

"My dear, we must welcome these people
to our shores. They have come all the way
from Spain. Scotland is not at war with
Spain, even if England is!"

"I will not go!" said the lady again. "And," she added, "I don't want you to go either."

At this the lord was angry. "I will go myself and bid these people welcome," he said, and he left her sitting in the room alone.

Then she was angry. "How dare he go and leave me here alone?" she thought.

When the lord reached Tobermory he found that a huge crowd had gathered. The great ship was sailing slowly into the bay. She was a sorry sight. Her masts had been broken and her sails had been ripped by the strong winds and seas.

The sailors launched small boats and rowed ashore. The lord of the castle went forward to greet them.

He shook hands with the captain, whose name was Don Ferreira. Beside him stood a beautiful lady. She had long dark hair. She had beautiful dark eyes. She wore a long dress. The lord thought that he had never seen anyone more beautiful. Here was the Spanish princess the messenger had told him about.

"Will you come and spend a few days at my castle and rest after your long voyage?" he asked. "My wife will be delighted to meet you."

The Spanish princess agreed, and the lord took her back with him to his castle. But his wife was not at all pleased to see the Spanish princess, although she pretended she was.

"Come in, my dear," she said. "You must be tired after your long voyage."

The Spanish princess did not speak English, so she only nodded her head and

smiled. The lady was very jealous when she
saw how enchanted her husband was by the
Spanish princess. He paid a great deal of
attention to her.

"I'll get my revenge," the lady said grimly
to herself.

So when the time came for the princess to
return to the ship, the lady decided to act.
She called upon the Witch of Mull to help her.

"Witch of Mull," she said, "I need your help."

"What can I do for you, your ladyship?"
asked the Witch of Mull.

"You can destroy the Spanish galleon and all aboard this very night!" said the lady. "I don't care what methods you use, as long as it's done tonight. I'll pay you handsomely for your efforts."

The Witch of Mull was astonished. But she bowed politely and left the room. "Good gracious me!" she said to her faithful black cat. "I always thought the lady of the castle was such a nice, good woman!"

Unfortunately the Witch of Mull was not a very efficient witch. She could make spells but they sometimes didn't work. However she decided the best thing to do was to cast a spell on the ship to make it sink.

She collected all the things she needed to make her spell. She mixed them all together in her cauldron and said the magic words. She did cause a boat to sink. But it was not the great Spanish galleon. It was a fishing boat with some men aboard. Without warning it sank to the bottom of the sea, and all the fishermen were drowned.

The Witch of Mull flew off to the mainland for a holiday because she knew that the lady of the castle would be very angry with her. She was right. The lady was furious! She called another witch.

"Blue-Eyed Witch of Lochaber!" she said. "I need your help."

"What is it, my lady?" asked the Blue-Eyed Witch of Lochaber.

"I want you to sink the Spanish galleon and all aboard her tonight!"

"But, my lady!" protested the Blue-Eyed Witch of Lochaber.

"Will you do it tonight? I'll pay you well," said the lady.

The Blue-Eyed Witch of Lochaber was surprised too. "Goodness gracious me," she said to her faithful ginger cat. "I thought the lady of the castle was a nice, good woman!"

She turned herself into a cormorant and flew to the place where the Spanish ship lay at anchor. Using her magic, she called upon all the brindled fairy cats of Mull. They came and sat in a circle all around her.

"Fairy cats," she said, "use your claws and your wits and your sharp, sharp teeth to destroy all aboard that great ship."

Then with a terrible shrieking and squealing all the brindled fairy cats clawed their way aboard the galleon. They stalked the sailors on the deck. They spat at the captain at the wheel. They growled at the ship's cats crouched in the corner. They pounced and ripped and clawed at everything they could see on that great ship, until the sailors were terrified and tried to run away.

Fairy cats, as you may know, have special
tails from which sparks fly when they are
angry. The largest of the cats chased a sailor
right down into the hold of the ship where
the gunpowder was stored. Suddenly a spark

from its tail set the gunpowder alight.

There was an enormous explosion. The whole ship blew up. Wreckage was scattered far and wide. Everyone on board was killed. And the remains of the Spanish galleon, with its treasure of gold, sank to the bottom of the sea in Tobermory Bay.

Many people have searched in vain for the treasure, but it has never been discovered.

When the proud and beautiful lady in the castle heard about the galleon she was delighted. But when her husband discovered that the Spanish princess was dead he was heartbroken.

The Blue-Eyed Witch of Lochaber flew to him and told him that his wife had ordered the destruction of the ship. He was horrified. He couldn't believe it at first.

For the rest of his life he never ever spoke to her again. And she died an unhappy woman, lonely and sad, sitting alone in her sitting room in the castle by the edge of the sea.

The Rugby Match

Dave, Mike, Ian and John were going to the International Rugby match between Scotland and Wales on Saturday. They had been looking forward to it for a long time.

Mike had his Scottish flag, the Lion Rampant, rolled up at the ready in the corner of his bedroom.

Ian had his tartan scarf neatly folded on his chest of drawers. His Mum had sewn a badge on. It said 'I'm proud to be a Scot'.

Dave had a special rosette made of tartan ribbon with a thistle in the middle. He was going to wear it on his jacket so that everyone would see that he was a Scottish supporter.

John had nothing particularly Scottish to wear. He was having trouble persuading his Mum to let him go.

"Stay and watch it on TV, John," she said. "You'll see it better that way."

"But, Mum," said John, "we got the tickets at school. I'll be in the schoolboys' enclosure. It's quite safe."

Reluctantly John's mother agreed. "Well, all right," she said. "But just be careful, will you?"

On the morning of the match the telephone rang. It was John's Granny. She had fallen and hurt herself and wanted John's Mum to go and help her.

John's Mum said, "I'm sorry, John, I know I said you could go, but that's Granny, and she needs me today. You stay and watch the match on TV and look after Andrew for me." Andrew was John's three-year-old brother.

"Aw, Mum, I want to go to the match!" John said in dismay.

"I can't help that," said his Mum. "Andrew needs to be looked after. You can go to the next one instead."

Dismally John watched her go to catch the bus. He switched on the TV set. It was *Grandstand*. The commentator was talking about the match. He said that Scotland had a good chance of winning today.

The door bell rang. It was Mike and Ian. They were ready to go.

"Come on John, we'll be late!" said Mike.

"I can't go," said John.

"Why not?" said Ian.

"My Mum's had to go and help my Granny, and I have to stay here and look after Andrew, so I'll just have to watch the

game on TV," John explained.

"That's AWFUL!" said Mike. "Dave can't come either because he's not feeling well. His Mum brought us his ticket in case we could sell it. And he sent you his rosette to wear."

"Me go too?" said Andrew hopefully.

"Good idea," said Ian. "We'll take him with us!"

"We can't do that," said John, "he's too wee."

"We'll take him in the pushchair," said Mike, " and he can have Dave's ticket."

"But Mum will have a fit when she finds out," said John, worried.

"She won't find out," said Ian.

"Come on," said Mike. "Get his coat. Hurry!"

"But ..." said John. Then he got Andrew's coat and gloves and found his pushchair. He made Andrew sit in it although he was a bit big for it.

"Sit down!" John told him. Andrew sat down.

Soon they were walking to the match. When they got to Murrayfield they had to stand in a queue to hand in their tickets through the turnstiles. The pushchair wouldn't go through. But a man lifted it over and they gave their tickets to the man at the gate.

John parked the pushchair near the gate and took Andrew's hand. They found their seats. Andrew sat down beside them. The band was marching up and down.

"Band," said Andrew. "Band."

Suddenly a man wearing a red and white scarf ran on to the field carrying a huge leek. He stuck it right in the middle of the rugby pitch and bowed down in front of it. The Welsh supporters shouted and cheered.

Then a man carrying a huge Scottish flag ran on to the pitch. He stuck the flag's stick in the ground and danced round it. The Scottish supporters shouted and cheered. Two policemen were walking towards the man with the flag. He pulled it out of the ground and ran away as fast as he could.

There was a roar from the crowd. The players were coming on to the field.

The Welsh team came running out first. They were wearing red and white strips. The Welsh supporters cheered. Then the Scottish team came running out in their blue strips. An enormous cheer went up. They ran about, throwing the ball to one another. John hoped that they would win the match.

Suddenly it went very quiet. The band played the Welsh national anthem. All the Welsh supporters sang in their own language. Then the band played *God Save the Queen*. Some of the Scottish supporters sang *Oh Flower of Scotland*, and some didn't sing at all. John thought *Oh Flower of Scotland* was a better song than *God Save the Queen* anyway. Then the match began.

Scotland got the ball first. They kicked it up to their half. Then a Welsh player got it and ran all the way back down the field again, dodging in and out of the Scottish players. He headed for the line and before he could be

stopped he had planted the ball behind the
goal. It was a try for Wales. The Scots clapped
politely but John felt disappointed. The
Welsh supporters cheered and cheered.
Andrew was frightened. He began to cry.

"Be QUIET!" said John. "It's OK. BE
QUIET!" Andrew was quiet.

After that Scotland seemed to play better,
but they didn't manage to score. Andrew got
down from his seat and started picking things

up off the ground.

Half-time came and the players stood eating their oranges and talking about their tactics for the second half.

The band began to play.

"Band," said Andrew eagerly. "Band." He stood up and watched them.

John wished he hadn't brought Andrew.

The second half started. The Scottish captain scored a drop goal in the first minute! Everyone jumped up and down. People hugged each other. It was wonderful!

Andrew cried again. John gave him the tartan rosette to play with.

The game became more exciting still. The Welsh captain scored a drop goal. Then Scotland scored a try. Silence fell as the captain ran to kick for a conversion. No one shouted out. The ball rose into the air and sailed right through the middle of the goalposts.

"Hurray! Hurray! Hurray!" shouted the three boys. The noise of cheering was deafening. The crowd stood up. Scotland was winning! The game went on.

Suddenly Ian said, "Where's Andrew?"

John and Mike looked round. He was not in his seat. He was not down on the ground. He was nowhere to be seen. John was horrified. He felt quite ill. What would his mother say? Andrew had vanished. He sat there feeling miserable. The Welsh supporters began to sing. Then suddenly, at the edge of the pitch, he saw a little figure running along. It was Andrew. He was heading for the band, who were sitting over on the far side of the pitch.

"There he is!" said John. He jumped down to the edge of the pitch and ran after Andrew.

"Sit down, lad, the match isn't over yet," said a voice behind him, but John paid no attention. He kept running until he caught up with Andrew. He grabbed him.

"Band," said Andrew. "Me see band." John held him tight. Andrew screamed.

"No, Andrew, no!" said John.

The Scottish pack were having a scrum very near their line. Then they scored a try! As the Scots cheered, Andrew wriggled free and ran off to see the band. John had to run after him. He got to him as Scotland scored again. The final whistle went and John found himself right at the entrance to the players' tunnel.

He held Andrew's hand tightly. Two big policemen were standing in front of him. The players ran off the pitch. John stretched out his hand. He managed to touch the Scottish captain on the arm.

"Great game!" he called. "Well done!"

The captain turned and smiled at him.
"Thanks very much. Glad you enjoyed it,"
he said, and then he ran into the tunnel and
disappeared with the others.

Holding Andrew's hand, John made his
way back to where he had left the pushchair.
He found it but could see no sign of his
friends. Pushing Andrew in his chair he
walked home by himself. He felt very pleased.
"Fancy me talking to the Scottish captain!"

he thought. When he got to his house he found Ian and Mike waiting for him.

"What happened?" they asked. So John told them all about chasing Andrew to the tunnel and getting caught in the crowd as the players ran off.

"I missed the final try because of Andrew, but if it hadn't been for him I wouldn't have had the chance to speak to the Scottish captain." They all looked at Andrew sitting in the pushchair still holding Dave's tartan rosette. He was fast asleep.

"Come round tomorrow," said John. "We'll watch the highlights on TV, and then I'll see the final try."

The next day Ian and Mike went round to John's house again. John's Mum and Dad sat down to watch too. Andrew was playing with his toys on the carpet in front of the TV set. The band began to play. Andrew got up.

"Band," he said, looking round at John. "Band," and pointed to the screen. John felt his face going red.

"That's right, Andrew," he said. "Band."
Then he whispered, "Be quiet!"

But Andrew would not be quiet. Mum had
to take him away to another room. The boys
and Dad settled down to watch the game.
John saw all the Scottish scores. After the
final one the whistle blew and he saw the
teams running off to the dressing rooms.
Then to his amazement he saw himself!
There he was, holding on to Andrew, talking to
the Scottish captain. Dad leaned forward in
his seat.

"Was that you there?" he asked John.

John's face was very red. "Yes," he said,

"that was me with Andrew. I had to look after him while Mum went to see Granny."

"We persuaded him," said Mike. "He wasn't going to go at all but we had an extra ticket for Andrew."

"He made me miss the final try but I got to speak to the Scottish captain," John told Dad.

"Does your mother know?" asked Dad.

"Not yet," said John. There was a pause. John was not sure what Dad would say. He thought he would be angry.

Suddenly Dad laughed. He laughed and laughed. Then he said, "I don't have to work on Saturdays any more. I'll look after Andrew the next time there's a match at Murrayfield. Right?"

Several weeks later John, Ian, Mike and Dave all set off to see Scotland play Ireland at Murrayfield. Dad looked after Andrew.

I wonder if Dad ever told Mum that Andrew had been at the rugby match?

Can you see the different colours of the Scottish and Welsh rugby supporters in the photograph on page 100? What are they? The national emblems of these two countries are shown on page 94. Why do you think such objects were chosen?

The club colours of the Scottish Rugby Union teams in the First Division are:

Ayr: pink, black and navy blue
Boroughmuir: navy blue and emerald green
Gala: maroon and white
Haddington: scarlet and navy blue
Hawick: green and white
Heriot's: navy blue and white
Jedforest: royal blue and white
Kelso: black and white
Kilmarnock: white, navy blue and red
Melrose: yellow and black
Selkirk: navy blue and white
Stewart's Melville: scarlet, black and gold
Watsonian: maroon and white
West of Scotland: red, yellow and navy

If you were designing a club strip, what colours would you make it? Draw a picture of your design.

Here are examples of club badges. Imagine your local club needs a new badge and think of a good design for it. The design should be based on things which local people will recognise.
You could add a motto to the badge, to encourage your club to play better!

Kelso

Melrose

Soldier's Leap

How far can you jump? Have you ever measured the distance? Is it one metre, or two, or even three?

This is a story about a man who jumped *five* metres over a whirlpool to get away from his enemy who was trying to kill him.

The place is called Soldier's Leap, and you can go and see it today. It is marked on the map of Scotland on page 110.

★   ★   ★   ★   ★

To understand this story it is a help to know a bit about the history of that time.

James II of England and VII of Scotland was a Catholic, but many of his subjects were not. He reigned for three years, from 1685–1688. At that time there was a great deal of unrest and rebellion in both England and Scotland.

Some Scots wanted James to stay on the throne. But the government had asked William of Orange and his wife Mary to be

king and queen. At a convention in Edinburgh
it was decided that Scotland would also
accept this arrangement. However many
Highlanders still supported James. They were
called Jacobites. Their leader was John
Graham of Claverhouse, Viscount Dundee.
General Hugh Mackay was the commander of
the government troops in Scotland.

The Jacobites had their base at Blair
Castle. This meant that they were in a good
position to keep control of the main road to

the north. The Pass of Killiecrankie lies near Blair Castle, and it was here that the Battle of Killiecrankie took place, in July 1689.

There were 2500 men in the Jacobite army. They wore no shoes and were used to sleeping out in the open wearing only their kilts and plaids. (At that time both kilt and plaid were one garment and this could be used as a blanket for sleeping in.) They carried shields and were armed with swords and muskets. They lined up on high ground, ready for battle.

The government had 3000 soldiers on foot and many more on horseback. But they had marched a long way and were weary. They had been issued with guns but had not had time to practise using them.

Viscount Dundee waited until the sun went down. Then he gave the order to attack. As was their custom, the Highlanders immediately took off their kilts and plaids and, wearing only their shirts and bonnets, rushed wildly at the government troops.

Before the troops had fired a few shots with their new guns, the Highlanders were upon them, fighting furiously. They broke the troops' lines, and began to chase them away!

There was a man called Donald MacBean on the government side. He had never fought before. He was terrified and wanted to get away as fast as he could. He caught sight of a riderless horse.

"I could get away on that fine beast," he thought to himself. He ran after it and managed to catch hold of the horse's mane. At that moment he saw a Highlander coming towards him, a dagger at the ready.

Quickly Donald MacBean put the horse's body between himself and the Highlander, for he knew the man would want the horse for himself. But the Highlander was quicker, for he dodged round to the far side of Donald MacBean, drew his musket from his belt and fired at him.

Luckily for Donald MacBean, it missed, and he ran away as fast as he could. The

Highlander chased him. Donald ran and ran,
jumping over rocks and boulders. He ran
until he reached a smooth high rock. There
he stopped in horror.

Below him was a whirlpool dark and deep.
He could not go back or to the left or to the
right. Safety lay only on the far bank, but
could he reach it?

There was no choice. He laid down his gun
and his hat. He took a deep breath and a
flying leap! The air whistled past his ears, his
stomach turned over as he came down, his
shoe fell off and a bullet whizzed past his left
ear.

With a shuddering jolt he landed on hard firm rock, a centimetre from the edge.

Tearing at the rock with his hands he scrambled up the side of the bank, away from the wild Highlander, away from the dark, evil water, away from the sound of battle.

He ran through trees and up a hill. He ran and ran until he came to a quiet field. There, sure he was no longer being followed, he sank down behind a dyke and had a rest, thankful to be alive.

The Highlander left on the high rock watched in amazement as Donald MacBean made his jump. It was he who had fired the shot. When Donald MacBean reached the far bank the Highlander tried another shot, but he was too far away. In disgust he threw the hat into the whirlpool and watched as the swirling water sucked it under and it disappeared.

The Highland army won that day. But their leader Viscount Dundee had been killed. The following month they regrouped to fight

Viscount Dundee

at Dunkeld. This time they were soundly
beaten and many men were killed. The
uprising against the government was over . . .
for the time being.

★　　★　　★　　★　　★

Next time you have music at school ask your
teacher to teach you the song about this piece
of history. The words were written by
Sir Walter Scott and they were later set to
music. The song is called *Bonnie Dundee*,
which was the nickname of Viscount Dundee.

To the Lords of Convention 'twas Claverhouse spoke,
  "'Ere the King's crown go down, there are
  crowns to be broke!
Then each cavalier who loves honour and me,
  Let him follow the bonnets o' Bonnie Dundee."

Chorus: Come fill up my cup and fill up my can,
      Come saddle my horses and call up my men;
      Unhook the west port and let us go free,
      For it's up wi' the bonnets o' Bonnie Dundee.

Dundee he is mounted, he rides up the street,
  The bells they ring backward, the drums they
  are beat,
But the Provost (douce man) said, "Just e'en let it be,
  For the toon is well rid o' that deil o' Dundee."

There are hills beyond Pentland and lands beyond
Forth,
    If there's lords in the south there are CHIEFS
    in the north;
There are brave Dunniewassals three thousand times three
    Will cry 'Hey for the bonnets o' Bonnie Dundee!'

Then awa' to the hills, to the lea, to the rocks,
    'Ere I own a usurper I'll crouch with the fox;
And tremble, false Whigs, in the midst o' your glee,
    Ye hae no seen the last o' my bonnets and me.

John's Funny Uncle

John's Uncle Bill was always being funny. He told lots of jokes.

"Have you heard the one about the sea monster?" he asked John one day.

"No," said John.

"What do sea monsters eat?" asked Uncle Bill.

"I don't know," said John. "What do sea monsters eat?"

"Fish and ships," said Uncle Bill, laughing.

"I know another one about a fish," said John.

"Let's hear it," said Uncle Bill.

"What kind of fish do you find in a bird cage?" asked John.

"I don't know," said Uncle Bill. "What kind of fish do you find in a bird cage?"

"A perch," said John, and they both laughed loudly.

"Here's another one," said Uncle Bill.

"What kind of fish is most useful on ice?"

John didn't know.

"A skate," said Uncle Bill. "Get it? It's a kind of fish too," he added.

"Oh, Bill," said Auntie Jill. "You've told that one a hundred times!"

"Well, here's one more just for luck," said Uncle Bill. "Have you heard the one about the kipper?"

"No," said John. "I don't think I've heard the one about the kipper."

"What fish terrorises other fish?" said Uncle Bill.

"I don't know," said John. "What fish terrorises other fish?"

"Jack the KIPPER!" said Uncle Bill, and he roared with laughter.

"Kippers, ugh," said Auntie Jill. "They make the house smell horrible."

"She doesn't appreciate my jokes," said Uncle Bill. "Never mind, come and I'll show you a good fast way of going downstairs."

He climbed to the top of the stairs and lay down on his front with his chin resting on the

top step. He stretched his arms
out and slid all the way
downstairs on his tummy.

"Now you do it,"
he told John.

So John slid all the
way downstairs on
his tummy, just
like Uncle Bill.
He arrived at the
bottom red-faced
and laughing.

Uncle Bill winked at John. "I'll show you
how to stand on your head," he said.

And that's just what he did.
He stood on his head for
five minutes.
John timed him
with his watch.

"Oh, Bill,' said Auntie Jill. "You're just showing off! You'll do yourself a mischief if you carry on like that."

She was right. The next day when John came home from school, his Mum told him that Uncle Bill had hurt his back and would have to stay in bed for a week. John hurried round to see him. He took him a comic and a bunch of grapes. Uncle Bill liked the comic because it made him laugh.

"Trouble is," he told John, "my back hurts when I laugh."

"How does it feel?" asked John.

"Better in bed," said Uncle Bill. "Don't worry, I'll be up and about in no time. Jill's quite right . . . serves me right for being a show-off." He leaned forward and whispered to John, "Could you maybe do me a favour?"

John nodded. "I'd like to, but what is it?" he asked.

"Remember that kipper joke? Do you think the next time you pass the fish shop you could go in and buy me a nice big fat juicy kipper for my tea?"

"But what will Auntie Jill say?" asked John.

"She'll be OK if *you* bring it. Here's some money. Keep the change."

The next day it rained and John's Mum came to collect him from school in the car. The day after that he had a half day and he walked home with his friends. He remembered about the kipper as they passed the fish shop. He went inside and bought a nice big fat juicy one. The fish man wrapped it in some paper for him.

When he got home he took it to his room.

"I'll parcel it up so it doesn't look like a kipper," he thought to himself.

He put some more paper round it. And then even more, so that it began to look square rather than fish-shaped. He wrote 'love from John' on a card and put it inside. He began to address the parcel to Uncle Bill. But he stopped and thought, "Uncle Bill will easily recognise my handwriting. How can I disguise it?"

Then he remembered that his father had received a parcel just that morning. The label said 'For the attention of Mr Fulton'. Dad and Uncle Bill were both called Mr Fulton because they were brothers. John found the wrapping paper from Dad's parcel and carefully cut the label off. Then he stuck it on the kipper parcel with sticky tape.

He carried it round to Uncle Bill's house and pushed the parcel through the letter-box. It landed with a soft thump at the other side of the door

John went home feeling pleased with himself. What a lovely surprise Uncle Bill would get when he opened the parcel!

Uncle Bill had been watching rather a lot of TV because of his sore back. He had a portable TV set beside his bed. He had been watching a film in which the hero was blown up by a bomb inside a parcel. It was a very good film and he had told Auntie Jill all about it.

When Auntie Jill came in at tea time she found the evening paper behind the door. Underneath it she was surprised to find the parcel. She thought it looked a bit suspicious. Could it be a parcel bomb like the one in the film? (The electricity meter was near the front door, and it made a ticking noise like a timing device in a bomb.)

She hurried upstairs to tell Uncle Bill. He had been sleeping.

"Bill," she said, "there's an odd parcel on the mat. I think it's ticking. Maybe it's a bomb!"

Uncle Bill yawned and sat up stiffly. "I'd better come and have a look," he said.

He slowly got up and hobbled to the front

door to see the parcel. He could hear the ticking noise too.

"Why on earth would anyone want to send me a bomb?" he wondered aloud.

"We'd better call the police," said Auntie Jill.

"Good idea," said Uncle Bill, and he
hobbled back to bed.

A policeman came. He took one look at the
parcel, heard the ticking noise and sent for
the Bomb Disposal Unit. They drove up in a
big van. They lifted the parcel very carefully
into the van. They drove away with it . . .

Auntie Jill was worried about the men from
the Bomb Disposal Unit. "They might get
blown up," she said.

"They're experts on these matters," said
Uncle Bill. "They'll be all right."

About an hour later the door bell rang.
Uncle Bill answered it. It was one of the men
from the Bomb Disposal Unit.

"Do you know anyone called John?" he
asked.

"Yes, I certainly do," said Uncle Bill.

"He sent you a kipper in the parcel. It isn't
a bomb after all. There's a card here with
'love from John' written on it."

"I don't believe it," said Uncle Bill and he
roared with laughter.

He phoned John straight away. "John," he
said. "Come round here straight away. I have
a very good joke to tell you."

John ran round to Uncle Bill's house as
fast as he could. He rang the bell and Auntie
Jill came to the door.

"Hallo, John," she said. "Come in and
hear the funniest fishy joke ever."

John went inside. The whole house smelled
of kipper frying.

Uncle Bill was still laughing. He told John
about the parcel on the mat, the policeman,
the Bomb Disposal Unit, and how they all
thought the parcel was a bomb.

"I parcelled it up like that so that Auntie

Jill wouldn't guess it was a kipper," said John. "And I used a label from Dad's parcel to confuse you too!"

"And I thought it was a bomb," said Auntie Jill. "It was that film on TV that did it."

"It's the best joke I've heard for a while," said Uncle Bill.

Then they all sat down and ate the kipper. It tasted delicious.